Mrs Wilde Sam Dino Eloise Kimba Lino Yoko Mr Byng

Are we quite sure we know how to drive this thing, Mrs Wilde?

Six lucky kids have won first prize in a geography competition. Now they and two of their teachers are off on an amazing journey around the world by hot-air balloon, exploring everywhere from the Statue of Liberty to the Taj Mahal, from the Eiffel Tower to the Great Wall of China. And you're invited!

But they do encounter some problems along the way... The balloon keeps blowing off course!

And every time the balloon lands, the kids scatter!

Your challenge is to find all six kids and the missing teacher in each destination. It's not as easy as it looks! There are a lot of kids wandering around who look very similar, except for the colour of a T-shirt, or different-coloured hair...

Now remember, kids, when we land it's very important that we stay together. You too, Mr Byng!

Although they might not always land in the right place, they have a wonderful time. (And to find out what the kids were supposed to learn on their trip around the world, turn to the back of the book, just before the solutions.)

BON VOYAGE!

BOLIVIA

Our first stop is Lake Titikaka in Bolivia. The guidebook says it's the highest lake in the world. Oh no—our balloon is caught in the treetops and everybody has fallen out! Now where have they all gone?

UP, UP and AWAY

A round-the-world puzzle adventure

SCOT RITCHIE

LITTLE HARE

This book is dedicated to my mother, who always lifted me up
—SR

Little Hare Books
4/21 Mary Street, Surry Hills
NSW 2010 AUSTRALIA
www.littleharebooks.com

Copyright © Scot Ritchie 2005

First published in 2005

National Library of Australia
Cataloguing-in-Publication entry

Ritchie, Scot.
Up, up and away : a round-the-world puzzle adventure.

For children.
ISBN 1 921049 01 4.

1. Picture puzzles - Juvenile literature. I. Title.

793.73

Designed by Serious Business
Produced by Phoenix Offset, Hong Kong
Printed in China

5 4 3 2 1

UNITED STATES

Next stop is the Statue of Liberty in New York. The statue was a birthday present from France to the United States on the anniversary of American independ— whoa! That strong wind has pushed us off course, and we've landed in the middle of a HUGE shopping mall! How am I going to find everyone?

CANADA

Now we're heading north to Canada and the CN Tower—one of the world's tallest buildings. There's the province of Quebec below us—but what's that music? It's an Autumn Fair! And that smell must be pies from the baking contest. I suppose we could stop for lunch...Where is everybody?!

ENGLAND

Across the Atlantic Ocean to London...
We'll visit the British Museum, which is the
oldest museum in the world— Crash! Oops.
I think we've landed in the wrong museum.
Come back!

DENMARK

Up, up and away to Copenhagen! Down below are the Tivoli Gardens. Built in 1843, this is Denmark's most popular tourist attraction. So, kids, shall we keep on going, or would you like to stop and try the rides?...Kids??

ITALY

In Rome, we can see an ancient building called the Pantheon—its walls are six metres thick! But what's that below? Ah, it's the ruins of a town that's over 1500 years old. Let's stop and take a look. Just make sure you stay...now where are they?

FRANCE

Now we're in Paris, so we must visit the Eiffel Tower. It was built in 1889 to commemorate the French Revolution. Let's just set down here and walk to the—hey! Stay together, kids!

EGYPT

A trip around the world just doesn't seem complete without a visit to the pyramids of Egypt. They're the only remaining structures of the seven wonders of the ancient world. History comes to life when you look out over them...Maybe too much life! Hey, kids, be careful!

CHINA

We're about to see one of the few human structures that's visible from outer space: the Great Wall of China. We'll just land here in this market in Beijing. But be careful; there are over one billion people in China, so don't get los— Oh, never mind.

THAILAND

When we get to Bangkok, I'll show you the Grand Palace. We can follow the Chao Phraya River. Did you know that many of Bangkok's inhabitants live on boats on this river? Wait a minute...What are you all doing down there?

INDIA

One of the most impressive sights in India is the Taj Mahal—a temple built by an emperor in memory of his beautiful wife. But why is that helicopter chasing us off? Oh, they're making a movie. And now the kids are in the middle of it!

AUSTRALIA

Our last stop: Sydney, Australia. Sydney's famous opera house was built in— Hey, what are we doing at the beach? Come on, kids, it's time to go home!

BOLIVIA

The original people of this area, the Incas, believed they originated from Lake Titikaka. They called the lake the "womb of mankind". It is one of the highest lakes in the world at 3820 metres (12 500 feet) above sea level. The air is thin up there!

CANADA

The CN Tower in Toronto is 553 metres (1815 feet) tall. Construction was completed in 1976, and it is still one of the tallest buildings in the world! And at 447 metres (1465 feet), the tower's observation deck, Sky Pod, is the world's highest.

DENMARK

The king of Denmark gave permission to Georg Carstensen to build an amusement park in the centre of Copenhagen for the enjoyment of the people. Tivoli Gardens, which opened in 1843, is now one of the oldest operating amusement parks in the world.

UNITED STATES

The Statue of Liberty, built in 1885, wasn't always known by that name. It was originally called "Liberty Enlightening the World". After building the statue in France it was taken apart (there were 350 pieces!) and shipped to the United States, where it was reassembled.

ENGLAND

The British Museum was founded in 1753. With the exception of the two World Wars, when some collections were removed for safety, the museum has stayed open continuously since then. It contains priceless artifacts from around the world.

ITALY

The Pantheon was built over 1800 years ago as a Roman temple, and was later consecrated as a Catholic church. Barges were used to transport the 60-tonne columns all the way from Egypt!

FRANCE

Every seven years the Eiffel Tower is painted dark brown. Sixty tonnes of paint are required! It was named after the contractor, Gustave Eiffel, and was built for the 1889 Universal Exhibition.

EGYPT

Built over 4000 years ago, the pyramids of Egypt were constructed as tombs for kings. Although the oldest of the seven wonders of the world, they are the only wonder still surviving.

CHINA

Originally the Great Wall of China was constructed as separate walls. Then, around 220 BC, Emperor Qin Shihuang unified them into one great wall, stretching about 6700 km (over 4100 miles).

THAILAND

The Grand Palace in Bangkok, which was finished in 1783, was the home of the royal family until 1946. The palace contains Thailand's most sacred temple and the beautiful Emerald Buddha.

INDIA

Construction of the Taj Mahal started the year after the Emperor's wife, Mumtaz Mahal, died in 1631 and was finished over 20 years later. To this day, the bodies of the Emperor and his wife lie under the building.

AUSTRALIA

Although the Sydney Opera House hasn't been around that long (construction was finished in 1973) it has become the icon of Australia around the world. It is one of the busiest performing arts centres in the world, with approximately 3000 events held there every year.

SOLUTIONS

BOLIVIA

UNITED STATES

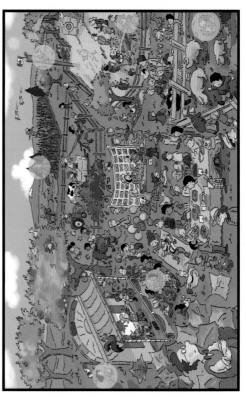

CANADA

ENGLAND

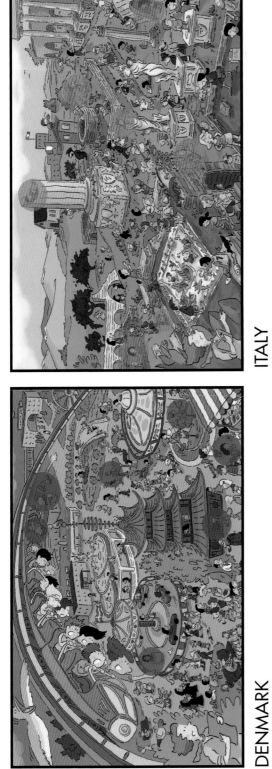

ITALY

EGYPT

DENMARK

FRANCE

THAILAND

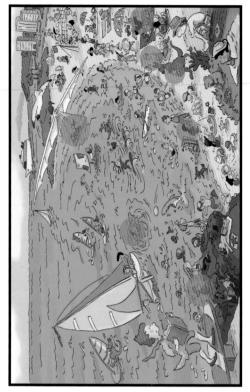

AUSTRALIA

CHINA

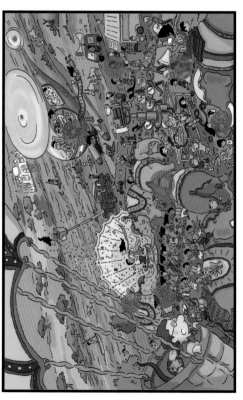

INDIA